DEMONS IN THE DARKNESS

LessonsForLifeBooks.com

IMPRINT A Cross Man Comics Adventure

Demons in the Darkness

© 2016 by
Keith M. Hammond
is published by
Lessons for Life Books, Inc.
St. Paul, MN 55116

Inquiries should be addressed in writing by email to:
permissionrequest@LessonsForLifeBooks.com

ISBN 13: 978-1938588983. Printed in the U.S.A.

Cover design and layout by Keith M. Hammond.
Story concept and 3D Illustrations by Keith M. Hammond.
NOTE: Several software applications and 3D models and 3D props were used to create and generate and render the scenes and characters contained within this and other Cross Man Comics adventures. All are used by purchase or permission.

CROSSMAN BOOKS

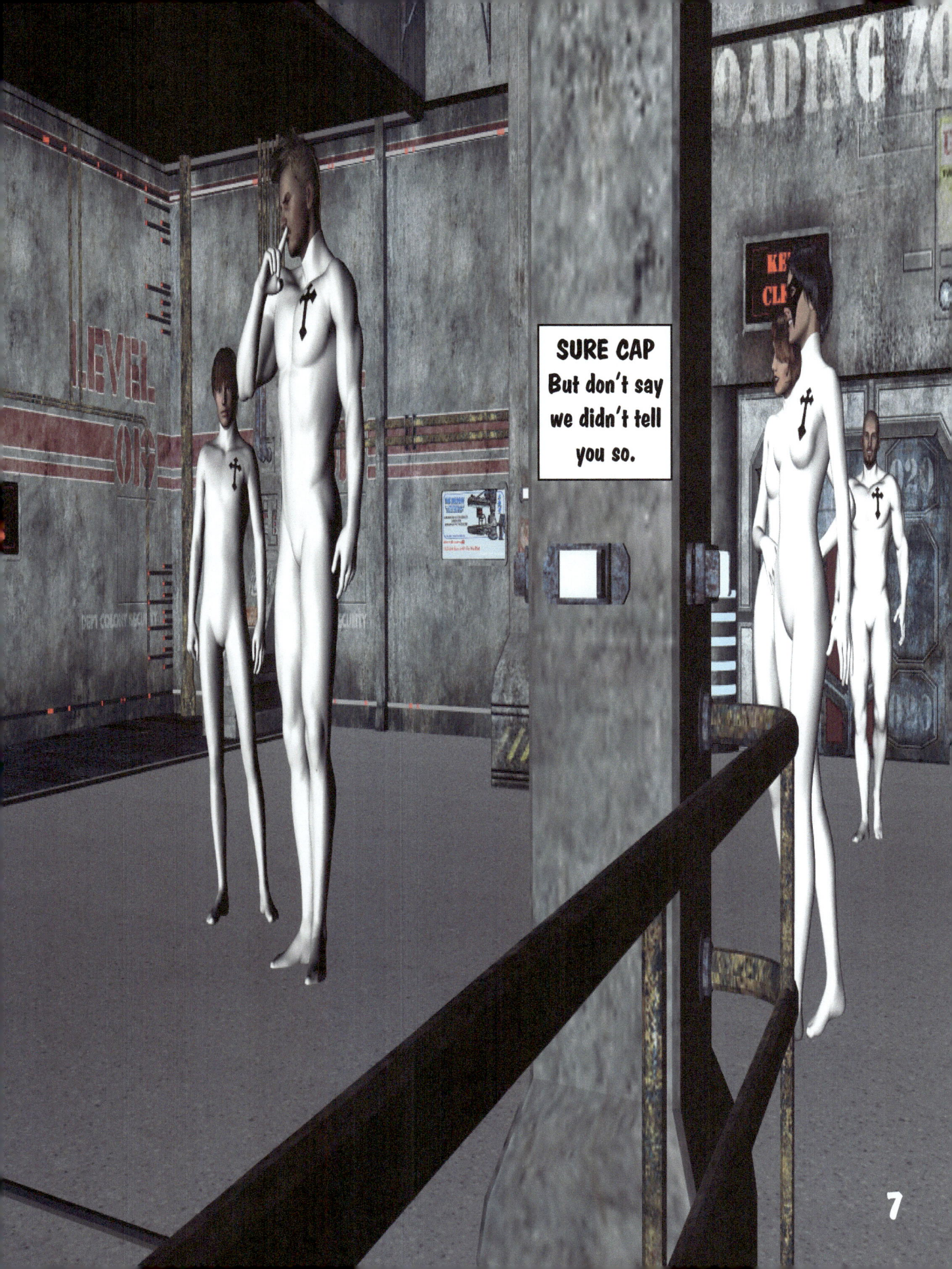

SURE CAP
But don't say
we didn't tell
you so.

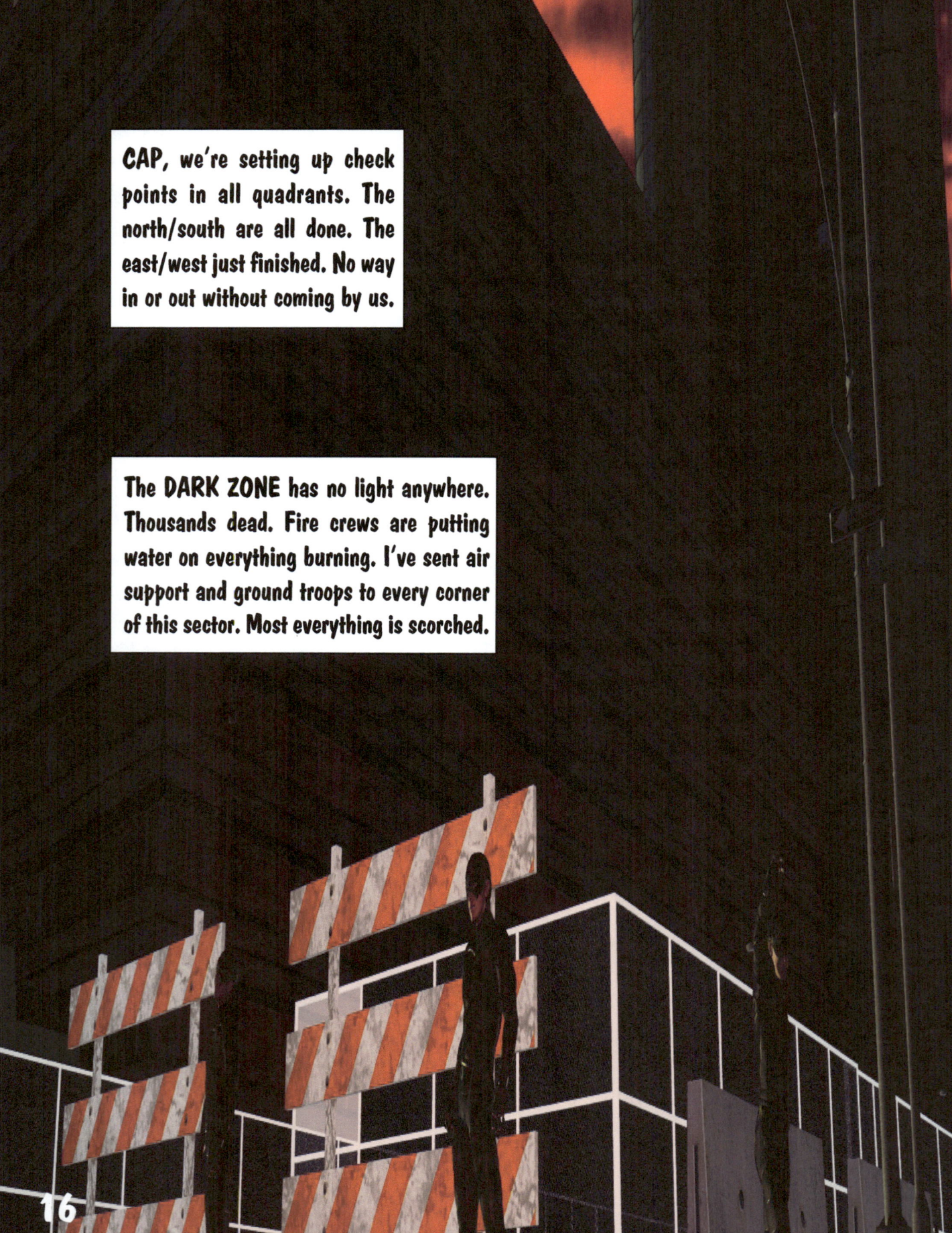

CAP, we're setting up check points in all quadrants. The north/south are all done. The east/west just finished. No way in or out without coming by us.

The DARK ZONE has no light anywhere. Thousands dead. Fire crews are putting water on everything burning. I've sent air support and ground troops to every corner of this sector. Most everything is scorched.

What's strange is that the city seems to have been...split...right...down...the...middle. One...side...dark...the...other...light.

I've...never...seen...anything...like...it.

YEAH, I see it. I have my team searching everywhere there's light.

STRENGTH was right. He smelled death before it rained down on us.

THE NEXT DAY...
Army Rangers have the dark zone surrounded. People who survived the firestorm keep coming to the edge of main street where the dark zone can be seen just steps away.

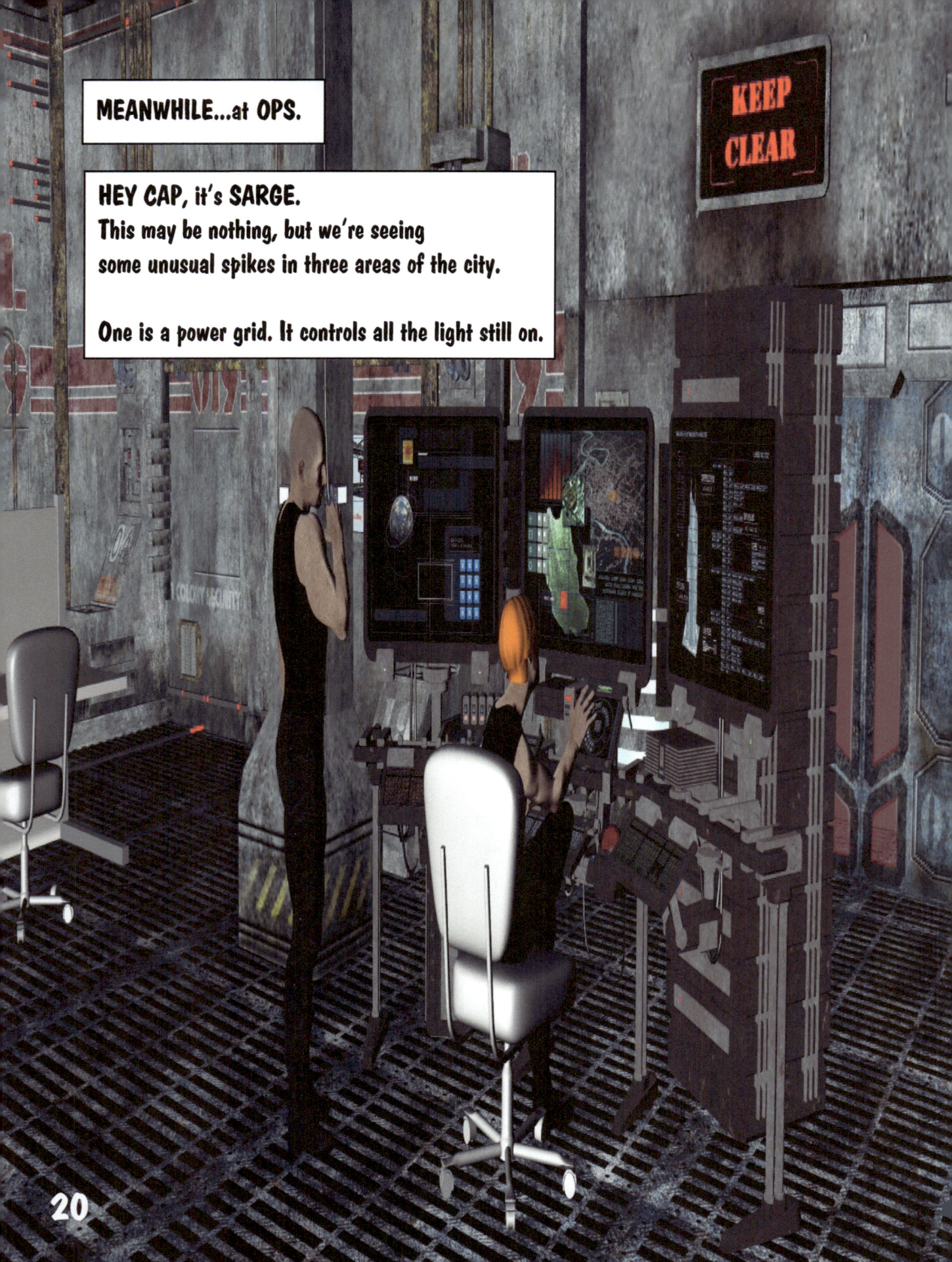

MEANWHILE...at OPS.

HEY CAP, it's SARGE.
This may be nothing, but we're seeing
some unusual spikes in three areas of the city.

One is a power grid. It controls all the light still on.

The second spike is a place that filters all the water in the area where all the light is left.

And CAP, the third location is the biggest food distribution center in the city. It's in an area where there's still light.

Three targets CAP. Light...Water...and Food.

22

Light...Water...Food.
SARGE that sounds like
something only Satan would do.

If he can KILL what's left of
the light, STEAL all the food,
and DESTROY the water...
he'll have control of the city.

I'm just arriving at the water
treatment facility. And I don't
see any people anywhere. This
is very strange. It's too quiet.

STRENGTH and FOX...
meet me here asap.

INTEL fires his water weapon toward the demon that is attacking SHADOW.

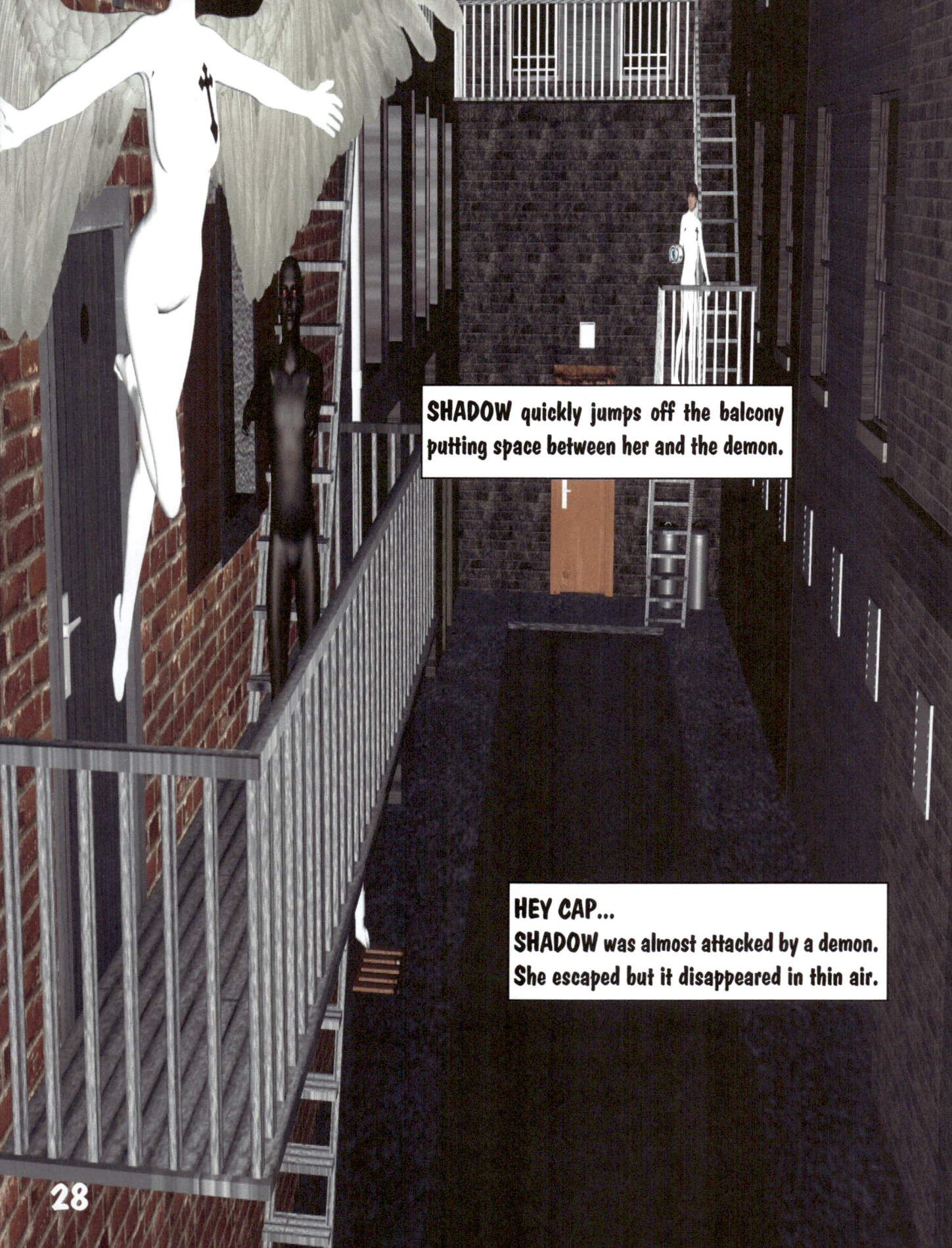

SHADOW quickly jumps off the balcony putting space between her and the demon.

HEY CAP...
SHADOW was almost attacked by a demon.
She escaped but it disappeared in thin air.

As INTEL and SHADOW arrive at the food center to meet up with the team, demons begin to surround them...

FOX and SHADOW head up to the catwalk. We'll take care of this level.

32

BACK AT OPS...

CAP it's **CIRCUIT**, I've located the source of the firestorm. A blaze bomb exploded inside a lava lake causing it to erupt. It's underneath an old vacant church at the edge of the city.

The level of the demonic activity there is off the scale! It was somehow hidden before, but now it's right there...out in the open.

And **CAP**...that church was demolished over 250 years ago, but it has somehow reappeared.

IN THE CENTER OF THE CITY
AN OLD HISTORIC CHURCH
HAS APPEARED EXACTLY
WHERE IT WAS DEMOLISHED
250 YEARS EARLIER.

In a dungeon deep underneath the church Satan and his den of demons gather.

I was the most beautiful angel ever created.
With the most precious jewels I was decorated.

I was given the sound of music and melody.
Creating rhythm and lyrics was my vanity.

Humans are pathetic and they are weak.
They know not how to truly ask, knock or seek.

They eat chemicals for food and poisons as drink.
Drugs for intoxication so that they cannot think.

They work to get rich even when God gives all they need.
Steal, kill and destroy one other all in the name of greed.

We will make God regret He ever created humanity.
We will make Him regret He gave them any authority.

They fall prey to fear and temptation.
And that will be our celebration.

God thinks He is victorious by banishing us from Heaven, but the battle has only just begun. Take to the streets and rule them, and in the end He will see the victory we have won!!!

Go and kill their light, steal their food, and destroy all the water that you can.

We will make Him remember the day He created the woman Eve and Adam the man.

Rise and come forth my dragon and prepare to devour all of our enemies.

When we return from the battle, we will bring you much to feed upon from our victory.

43

CAP, be careful when you get to that church, sensors show a very large animal presence there!

45

The entire edifice is empty, but it is eerie and evil is everywhere.

HEY SARGE, after I remove Satan from underneath this place, send your rangers to blow it to bits. Making this concrete implode should cover over the lava lake.

48

AND CIRCUIT, find out how this building appeared again 250 years after it was demolished.

DRAGON, this is the day that you shall DIE!!!

As **CAPTAIN CROSS** concentrates on killing the carnivore...

CAP steadies his steel sword to strike and is determined to defeat the dragon.

See much more of this epic battle in PART TWO
of the next adventure of Cross Man - Demons in the Darkness!